Frederick Locker-Lampson

London rhymes

Frederick Locker-Lampson

London rhymes

ISBN/EAN: 9783337261030

Printed in Europe, USA, Canada, Australia, Japan

Cover: Foto ©Andreas Hilbeck / pixelio.de

More available books at **www.hansebooks.com**

LONDON RHYMES.

LONDON RHYMES

BY

FREDERICK LOCKER

FIFTH AMERICAN EDITION

NEW YORK
FREDERICK A. STOKES COMPANY
MDCCCXC

PUBLISHERS' NOTE.

Frederick A. Stokes Company take pleasure in stating that they are Mr. Locker's authorized publishers in the United States. This edition is the AUTHOR'S EDITION, selected and revised by him.

CONTENTS.

ADVICE TO A POET.

Now if you'll only take, perchance,
But half the pains to learn, that we
Still take to hide our ignorance—
How very clever you will be!

Dear Poet, do not rhyme at all!
   But if you must, don't tell your neighbours,
Or five in six, who cannot scrawl,
   Will dub you "donkey" for your labours.
This epithet may seem unjust
   To you, or any Verse-begetter:—
Must we admit, I fear we must,
   That nine in ten deserve no better?

Then let them bray with leathern lungs,
   And match you with the beast that grazes;
Or wag their heads, and hold their tongues,
   Or damn you with the faintest praises.

B

Be patient, for be sure you won't
  Win vogue without extreme vexation :
And hope for sympathy,—but don't
  Expect it from a near relation.

When strangers first approved my books,
  My kindred marvell'd what the praise meant ;
They now wear more respectful looks,
  But can't get over their amazement.
Indeed, they've power to wound beyond
  That wielded by the fiercest hater,
For all the time they are so fond—
  Which makes the aggravation greater.

       *   *   *   *

Most warblers only half express
  The threadbare thoughts they feebly **utter** :
Now if they tried for something less
  They might not sink, and gasp, and flutter.
Fly low at first,—then mount and win
  The niche for which the town's contesting ;
And never mind your kith and kin,—
  But never give them cause for jesting.

Hold Pegasus in hand, control
    A taste for ornament ensnaring;
Simplicity is yet the soul
    Of all that Time deems worth the sparing.
Long lays are not a lively sport,
    So clip your own to half a quarter;
If readers now don't think them short,
    Posterity will cut them shorter.

       *   *   *   *

I look on bards who whine for praise
    With feelings of profoundest pity:
They hunger for the Poet's bays,
    And swear one's waspish when one's witty.
The critic's lot is passing hard, —
    Between ourselves, I think reviewers,
When call'd to truss a crowing bard,
    Should not be sparing of the skewers.

       *   *   *   *

We all, the foolish and the wise,
    Regard our verse with fascination,
Through asinine-paternal eyes,
    And hues of Fancy's own creation;

Prythee, then, check that passing sneer
   At any self-deluded rhymer
Who thinks his beer (the smallest beer!)
   Has all the gust of *all Hochheimer.*

     *   *   *   *

Oh, for the Poet-Voice that swells
   To lofty truths, or noble curses—
I only wear the cap and bells,
   And yet some Tears are in my verses.
I softly trill my sparrow reed,
   Pleased if but one should like the twitter;
Humbly I lay it down to heed
   A music or a minstrel fitter.

MY MISTRESS'S BOOTS.

She has dancing eyes and ruby lips,
Delightful boots—and away she skips.

They nearly strike me dumb,—
I tremble when they come
    Pit-a-pat :
This palpitation means
These Boots are Geraldine's—
    Think of that !

O, where did hunter win
So delicate a skin
    For her feet ?
You lucky little kid,
You perish'd, so you did,
    For my Sweet.

The faery stitching gleams
On the sides, and in the seams,
    And reveals

That the Pixies were the wags
Who tipt these funny tags,
  And these heels.

What soles to charm an elf!—
Had Crusoe, sick of self,
  Chanced to view
One printed near the tide,
O, how hard he would have tried
  For the two !

For Gerry's debonair,
And innocent and fair
  As a rose ;
She's an Angel in a frock,
She's an Angel with a clock
  To her hose !

The simpletons who squeeze
Their pretty toes to please
  Mandarins,
Would positively flinch
From venturing to pinch
  Geraldine's.

Cinderella's *lefts and rights*
To Geraldine's were frights:
    And I trow
The Damsel, deftly shod,
Has dutifully trod
    Until now.

Come, Gerry, since it suits
Such a pretty Puss (in Boots)
    These to don,
Set your dainty hand awhile
On my shoulder, Dear, and I'll
    Put them on.

ALBURY: *June* 29, 1864.

THE REASON WHY.

Ask why I love these roses fair,
And whence they come, and whose they were;
They come from her, and not alone,—
They bring her sweetness with their own.

Or ask me why I love her so;
I know not: this is all I know,
These roses bud and bloom, and twine
As she round this fond heart of mine.

And this is why I love these flowers,
Once they were hers, they're mine—they're ours!
I love her, and they soon will die,
And now you know the Reason Why.

TEMPORA MUTANTUR!

Yes, here, once more a traveller,
   I find the Angel Inn,
Where landlord, maids, and serving-men
   Receive me with a grin:
Surely they can't remember Me,
   My hair is grey and scanter;
I'm changed, so changed since I was here—
   O tempora mutantur!

The Angel's not much alter'd since
   The happy month of June,
That brought me here with Pamela
   To spend our honeymoon:
Ah me, I even recollect
   The shape of this decanter!
We've since been both much put about—
   O tempora mutantur!

Ay, there's the clock, and looking-glass
 Reflecting me again ;
She vow'd her Love was very fair,
 I see I'm very plain :
And there's that daub of Prince Leeboo;
 'Twas Pamela's fond banter
To fancy it resembled *me*—
 O tempora mutantur!

The curtains have been dyed, but there,
 Unbroken, is the same—
The very same—crack'd pane of glass
 On which I scratch'd her name.
Yes, there's her tiny flourish still ;
 It used to so enchant her
To link two happy names in one—
 O tempora mutantur!

  * * * *

The pilgrim sees an empty chair
 Where Pamela once sat ;
It may be she had found her grave,
 It might be worse than that :

The fairest fade, the best of men
Have met with a supplanter ;—
I wish that I could like this cry
Of tempora mutantur.

A WINTER FANTASY.

Your veil is thick, and none would know
   The pretty face it quite obscures;
But if you foot it through the snow,
   Distrust those little Boots of yours.

The tell-tale snow, a sparkling mould,
   Says where they go and whence they came,
Lightly they touch its carpet cold,
   And where they touch they sign your name.

She pass'd beneath yon branches bare:
   How fair her face, and how content !
I only know her face was fair,—
   I only know she came and went.

Pipe, robins, pipe ; though boughs be bleak
   Ye are her winter choristers ;
Whose cheek will press that rose-cold cheek ?
   What lips those fresh young lips of hers ?

THE HOUSEMAID.

The poor can love through toil and pain,
Although their homely speech is fain
    To halt in fetters:
They feel as much, and do far more
Than some of those they bow before,
    Miscall'd their betters.

Wistful she stands—and yet, resign'd,
She watches by the window-blind :
    Poor Girl.   No doubt
The passers-by despise thy lot :
Thou canst not stir, because 'tis not
    Thy *Sunday out.*

To play a game of hide and seek
With dust and cobweb all the week
    Small pleasure yields :
Oh dear, how nice it were to drop
One's pen and ink—one's pail and mop ;
    And scour the fields.

Poor Bodies few such pleasures know ;
Seldom they come.   How soon they go !
    But Souls can roam ;
For, lapt in visions airy-sweet,
She sees in this unlovely street
    Her far-off home.

The street is now no street ! She pranks
A purling brook with thymy banks.
    In Fancy's realm
Yon post supports no lamp, aloof
It spreads above her parents' roof,—
    A gracious elm.

A father's aid, a mother's care,
And life for her was happy there :
    But here, in thrall
She waits, and dreams, and fondly dreams,
And fondly smiles on One who seems
    More dear than all.

Her dwelling-place I can't disclose !
Suppose her fair, her name suppose
    Is *Car*, or *Kitty* ;

She may be *Jane*—she might be plain—
For must the Subject of my strain
   Be always pretty?

     *   *   *

Oft on a cloudless afternoon
Of budding May and leafy June,
   Fit Sunday weather,
I pass thy window by design,
And wish thy Sunday out and mine
   Might fall together.

For sweet it were thy lot to dower
With one brief joy: a white-robed flower
   That prude or preacher
Hardly could deem it were unmeet
To lay on thy poor path, thou sweet,
   Forlorn young Creature.

     *   *   *

But if her thought on wooing run
And if her Sunday-Swain is one
   Who's fond of strolling,
She'd like my nonsense less than his,
And so it's better as it is—
   And that's consoling.

1861.

TO MY OLD FRIEND POSTUMUS.

(J. G.)

And, like yon clocke, when twelve shalle so—se
 To call our soules away,
Together may our hands be found,
 An earnest that we praie.

My Friend, our few remaining years
 Are hasting to an end,
They glide away, and lines are here
 That time can never mend ;
Thy blameless life avails thee not,—
 Alas, my dear old Friend !

Death lifts a burthen from the poor,
 And brings the weary rest ;
But oft from earth's green orchard trees
 The canker takes our best—
The Well-beloved ! she bloom'd, and now
 The turf is on her breast.

O pleasant Earth ! This peaceful home !
  The darling at my knee !
My own dear wife ! Thyself, old Friend !
  And must it come to me,
That any face shall fill my place
  Unknown to them and thee ?

Ay, vainly are we fenced about
  From peril, day and night ;
Those awful rapids must be shot,
  Altho' our skiff be slight ;
O, pray that then we may descry
  Some cheering beacon-light.

HEINE TO HIS MISTRESS.

What do the violets ail,
  So wan, so shy?
Why are the roses pale?
  Oh why? Oh why?

The lark sad music makes
  To sullen skies;
From yonder flowery brakes
  Dead odours rise.

Why is the sun's new birth
  A dawn of gloom?
Oh why is this fair earth
  My joyless tomb?

I wait apart and sigh,
  I call to thee;
Why, Heart's-beloved, why
  Didst thou leave me?

1876.

ON "A PORTRAIT OF A LADY."

BY THE PAINTER.

I gathered it wet for my own sweet Pet
As we whisper'd and walk'd apart:
She gave me that rose, it is fragrant yet,—
And oh, it is near my heart.

She is good, for she must have a guileless mind
    With that noble, trusting air ;
A rose with a passionate heart is twined
    In her crown of golden hair.
Some envy the cross that caressingly dips
    In her bosom, and some had died
For the promise of bliss on her red, red lips,
    And her thousand charms beside.

She is lovely and good ; she has peerless eyes ;
    A haunting shape.   She stands
In a blossoming croft, under kindling skies,—
    The weirdest of faery lands ;

There are sapphire hills by the far-off seas,
   Grave laurels, and tender limes ;
They tremble and glow in the morning breeze, -
   My Beauty is up betimes.

A bevy of idlers press around,
   To wonder, and wish, and loll ;
" Now who is the painter, and where has he found
   The Woman we all extol,
With her fresh young mouth, and her candid brow,
   And a bloom as of bygone days ?"—
How natural sounds their worship, how
   Impertinent seems their praise !

I stand aloof; I can well afford
   To pardon the babble and crush
As they praise a work (do I need reward ?)
   That has grown beneath my brush :
Aloof—and in fancy again I hear
   The music clash in the hall,
When they crown'd her Queen of their dance and
      cheer,
   —She is mine, and Queen of all !

Yes, my thoughts are away to that happy day,
　A few short months agone,
When we left the games, and the dance, to stray
　Through the dewy flowers, alone.
My feet are again among flowers divine,
　Away from the noise and glare,
When I kiss'd her mouth, and her lips press'd
　　mine,
　And I fasten'd that rose in her hair.
　1868.

At Susan's name the fancy plays
With chiming thoughts of early days,
  And hearts unwrung:
When all too fair our future smiled,
When she was Mirth's adopted child,
  And I was young.

    *   *   *   *

And summer smiles, but summer spells
Can never charm where sorrow dwells—
  No maiden fair,
Or sad, or gay, the passer sees,—
And still the much-loved elder-trees
  Throw shadows there.

Her quiet resting-place is far away;
  None dwelling there can tell you her sad story.
The stones are mute.   The stones could only say,
  " A humble Spirit pass'd away to glory."

She loved the murmur of this mighty town;
  The lark rejoiced her from its lattice prison;
And now her grave is green—her bird has flown,—
  Some dust is waiting—a glad Soul has risen.

No city smoke to stain the heather bells;
  Sigh, gentle winds, around my lone Love sleep-
     ing;
She bore her burthen here, but now she dwells
  Where scorner cannot come, and none are
     weeping.

My name was falter'd with her parting breath;
  These arms were round my Darling at the latest:
All scenes of death are woe, but painful death
  In those we dearly love is woe the greatest.

I could not die; HE will'd it otherwise:
  My lot is here, and sorrow, wearing older,
Weighs down the heart, but does not fill the eyes, —
  Even my friends may think that I am colder.

But when at times I steal away from these,
  To find her Grave, and pray to be forgiven,
And when I watch beside her on my knees,
  I think I am a little nearer Heaven.
    1861.

THE BEAR PIT.

IN THE ZOOLOGICAL GARDENS.

*It seems that poor Bruin has never had peace
'Twixt bald men in Bethel, and wise men in grease.*
                                        OLD ADAGE.

We liked the Bear's serio-comical face,
As he loll'd with a lazy, a lumbering grace ;
Said Slyboots to me (as if *she* had got none),
"Papa, let's give Bruin a bit of your bun."

Says I, "A plum bun might please wistful old
        Bruin,
He can't eat the stone that the cruel boy threw in ;
Stick *yours* on the point of mamma's parasol,
And then he will climb to the top of the pole.

"Some Bears have got two legs, and some have
        got more,
Be good to old Bears if they've no legs or four ;
Of duty to age you should never be careless,—
My dear, I am bald, and I soon may be hairless !

" The gravest aversion exists among Bears
From rude forward persons who give themselves
    airs,
We know how some graceless young people were
    maul'd
For plaguing a Prophet, and calling him *bald.*

" Strange ursine devotion ! Their dancing-days
    ended,
Bears die to ' remove ' what, in life, they defended :
They succour'd the Prophet, and, since that affair,
The bald have a painful regard for the boar."

My MORAL ! Small people may read it, and run.
(The Child has my moral,—the Bear has my bun.)

UNREFLECTING CHILDHOOD.

The world would lose its finest joys
Without its little girls and boys ;
Their careless glee, and simple ruth,
And trust, and innocence, and truth.
—Ah, what would your poor poet do
Without such little folk as you ?

It is indeed a little while
　　Since you were born, my happy Pet ;
Your future beckons with a smile,
　　Your bygones don't exist as yet.
Is all the world with beauty rife ?
　　Are you a little Bird that sings
Her simple gratitude for life,
　　　　And lovely things ?

The ocean, and the waning moons,
　　And starry skies, and starry dells,
And winter sport, and golden Junes,
　　Art, and divinest Beauty-spells :

Festa, and song, and frolic wit,
   And banter, and domestic mirth,—
They all are ours ! dear Child, is it
      A pleasant earth ?

And poet friends, and poesy,
   And precious books, for any mood :
And then—that best of company—
   Those graver thoughts in solitude
That hold us fast and never pall :
   Then there is You, my Own, my Fair—
And I . . . soon I must leave it all,
      —And much you care.

THE OLD STONEMASON.

A showery day in early spring,
  An Old Man and a Child
Are seated near a scaffolding,
  Where marble blocks are piled.

His clothes are stain'd by age and soil,
  As hers by rain and sun ;
He looks as if his days of toil
  Were very nearly done.

To eat his dinner he had sought
  A staircase proud and vast,
And here the duteous Child had brought
  His scanty noon repast.

A worn-out Workman needing aid ;
  A blooming Child of Light ;
The stately palace steps ;—all made
  A most pathetic sight.

We had sought shelter from the storm,
    And saw this lowly Pair,—
But none could see a Shining Form
    That watch'd beside them there.

1674.

THE MUSIC PALACE.

Shall you go? I don't ask you to seek it or shun it;
I went on an impulse: I've been and I've done it.

So this is a Music-hall, easy and free,
A temple for singing, and dancing, and *spree*;
The band is at *Faust*, and the benches are filling,
And all that I have can be had for a shilling.

The senses are charm'd by the sights and the
        sounds;
A spirit of affable gladness abounds:
With zest we applaud, and as madly recall
The singer, the *cellar-flap-dancer*, and all.

What vision comes on with a wreath and a lyre?
A creature of impulse in scanty attire;
She plays the good sprite in a dream-haunted
        dell,
She has ankles! and eyes like a wistful gazelle.

A clown sings a song, and a droll cuts a caper,
And then she dissolves in a rose-colour'd vapour :
Then an imp on a rope is a painfully-pleasant
Sensation for all the mammas that are present.

But who is the Damsel that smiles to me there
With so reckless, indeed, so defiant an air?
She is bright—that she's pretty is more than I'll
　　say.
Is she happy?　At least she's exceedingly gay.

　　　　＊　　　＊　　　＊　　　＊　　　＊

It seems to me now, as we pass up the street,
Is Nell worse than I, or the worthies we meet?
She is reckless, her conduct's exceedingly sad—
A coin may be light, but it need not be bad.

Heaven help thee, poor Child : now a graceless
　　　　and gay Thing,
You once were your Mother's, her pet and her
　　　　plaything :
Where was your home?　Are the stars that look
　　　　down
On that home, the cold stars of this pitiless Town?

The stars are a riddle we never may read,
I prest her poor hand, and I bade her *Godspeed!*
She left me a heart overladen with sorrow—
You may hear Nelly's laugh at the palace to-
   morrow !

Ah ! some go to revel, and some go to rue,
For some go to ruin.   There's Paul's tolling two.

MRS. SMITH.

Heigh-ho ! they're wed.   The cards are dealt,
— Our frolic games are o'er ;
I've laugh'd, and fool'd, and loved.   I've felt—
As I shall feel no more !
Yon little thatch is where she lives,
Yon spire is where she met me ;—
I think that if she quite forgives,
She cannot quite forget me.

Last year I trod these fields with Di,—
Fields fresh with clover and with rye ;
    They now seem arid :
Then Di was fair and single ; how
Unfair it seems on me, for now
    Di's fair—and married !

A blissful swain—I scorn'd the song
Which tells us though young Love is strong,
    The Fates are stronger :
Then breezes blew a boon to men,
The buttercups were bright, and then
    This grass was longer.

D

That day I saw and much esteem'd
Di's ankles, that the clover seem'd
 Inclined to smother :
I twitch'd, and soon untied (for fun)
The ribbon of her shoes, first one,
 And then the other.

I'm told that Virgins augur some
Misfortune if their shoe-strings come
 To grief on *Friday:*
And so did Di, and then her pride
Decreed that shoe-strings so untied
 Are "so untidy!"

Of course I knelt; with fingers deft
I tied the right, and tied the left :
 Says Di, "This stubble
Is very stupid !—as I live
I'm quite ashamed !. . . I'm shock'd to give
 You so much trouble !"

For answer I was fain to sink
To what we all would say and think
 Were Beauty present :

"Don't mention such a simple act—
A trouble? not the least! In fact
    It's rather pleasant!"

I trust that Love will never tease
Poor little Di, or prove that he's
    A graceless rover.
She's happy now as *Mrs. Smith*—
And less polite when walking with
    Her chosen lover!

Heigh-ho! Although no moral clings
To Di's blue eyes, and sandal strings,
    We've had our quarrels.
I think that Smith is thought an ass,—
I know that when they walk in grass
    She wears *balmorals.*

1864.

TO LINA OSWALD.

(WITH A BIRTHDAY LOCKET.)

" My Darling wants to see you soon,"—
  I bless the little Maid, and thank her;
To do her bidding, night and noon
  I draw on Hope—Love's kindest banker!

Your Sun is in brightest apparel,
  Your birds and your blossoms are gay,
But where is my jubilant carol
  To welcome so joyous a day?
I sang for you when you were smaller,
  As fair as a fawn, and as wild :
Now, Lina, you're ten and you're taller—
  You elderly child.

I knew you in shadowless hours,
  When thought never came with a smart ;
You then were the pet of your flowers,
  And joy was the child of your heart.

I ever shall love you, and dearly !
  I think when you're even thirteen
You'll still have a heart, and not merely
      A flirting machine !   -

And when time shall have spoil'd you of passion,
  Discrown'd what you now think sublime,
Oh, I swear that you'll still be the fashion,
  And laugh at the antics of Time.
To love you will then be no duty ;
  But happiness nothing can buy—
There's a bud in your garland, my Beauty,
      That never can die.

A heart may be bruised and not broken,
  A soul may despair and still reck ;
I send you, dear Child, a poor token
  Of love, for your dear little neck.
The heart that will beat just below it
  Is open and pure as your brow—
May that heart, when you come to bestow it,
      Be happy as now.

1869—1872.

THE OLD GOVERNMENT CLERK.

(OLD STYLE.)

A kindly good Man, quite a stranger to fame,
  His heart still is green, tho' his head shows a hour lock;
Perhaps his particular star is to blame,—
  It may be he never took Time by the forelock.

We knew an old Scribe, it was "once on a time,"
  An era to set sober datists despairing :
Then let them despair ! Darby sat in a chair
  Near the Cross that gave name to the Village of
    Charing.

Though silent and lean, Darby was not malign,
  What hair he had left was more silver than sable ;
He had also contracted a curve in the spine,
  From bending too constantly over a table.

His pay and expenditure, quite in accord,
  Were both on the strictest economy founded ;

His rulers were known as the Sealing-wax Board,—
They ruled where red-tape and snug places
abounded.

In his heart he look'd down on this dignified Knot ;
And why? The forefather of one of these
senators—
A rascal concern'd in the Gunpowder Plot—
Had been barber-surgeon to Darby's progenitors.

Poor fool ! is not life a vagary of luck ?
For thirty long years of genteel destitution
He'd been writing despatches ; which means he
had stuck
Some heads and some tails to much circumlo-
cution.

This sounds rather weary and dreary ; but, no !
Though strictly inglorious, his days were
quiescent ;
His red-tape was tied in a true-lover's bow
Every night when returning to Rosemary
Crescent.

There Joan meets him smiling, the Young Ones
 are there ;
 His coming is bliss to the half-dozen wee Things ;
The dog and the cat have a greeting to spare,
 And Phyllis, neat-handed, is laying the tea-things.

East wind, sob eerily ! Sing, kettle, cheerily !
 Baby's abed, but its Father will rock it ;—
His little ones boast their permission to toast
 That cake the good fellow brings home in his
  pocket.

This greeting the silent Old Clerk understands,
 Now his friends he can love, had he foes he could
  mock them ;
So met, so surrounded, his bosom expands,—
 Some hearts have more need of such homes to
  unlock them.

And Darby at least is resign'd to his lot ;
 And Joan, rather proud of the sphere he's
  adorning,
Has well-nigh forgotten that Gunpowder Plot,—
 And *he* won't recall it till ten the next morning.

A day must be near when, in pitiful case,
  He will drop from his *Branch*, like a fruit more
    than mellow ;
Is he yet to be found in his usual place?
  Or is he already forgotten ? Poor Fellow !

If still at his duty he soon will arrive ;
  He passes this turning because it is shorter ;
He always is here as the clock's going five !—
  Where is He? . . Ah, it is chiming the quarter !
  1835.

OLD LETTERS.

Have sorrows come?   Has pleasure sped?
Is earthly bliss an empty bubble?
Is some one dull, or something dead?
O may I, mayn't I share your trouble?

*   *   *

Ay, so it is, and is it fair?
Poor men (your elders and your betters!)
Who can't look pretty in despair,
Feel quite as sad about their letters.
                              HER LETTERS.

Old letters ! wipe away the tear
  For vows and hopes so vainly worded ;
A Pilgrim finds his Journal here
  Since first his youthful loins were girded.

Yes, here are scrawls from Clapham Rise ;
  Do mothers still their schoolboys pamper ?
Oh how I hated Dr. Wise !
  Oh how I loved a well-fill'd hamper !

How strange to commune with the Dead !
   Dead Joys, dead Loves.   Wan leaves—how
      many
From Friendship's tree untimely shed—
   And here is one, ah, sad as any ;

A ghastly bill ! " *I disapprove.*"
   And yet She help'd me to defray it :
What tokens of a Mother's love !
   O bitter thought,—I can't repay it.

And here's the offer that I wrote
   In '33 to Lucy Diver ;
And here John Wylie's begging note,—
   He never paid me back a stiver.

And here my feud with Major Spike ;
   That bet about the French Invasion :—
I must confess I acted like
   A simpleton on that occasion.

Here's news from Paternoster Row ;
   How mad I was when first I learnt it !
They would not take my Book, and now
   I wish to goodness I had burnt it.

And here's a score of notes at last,
  With "*Love*" and "*Dove,*" and "*Sever—Never*";
Though hope, though passion may be past,
  Their perfume seems, ah, sweet as ever.

A Human Heart should beat for two,
  Whate'er may say your single scorners;
And all the Hearths I ever knew
  Had got a Pair of chimney-corners.

See here a double violet—
  Two locks of hair—A deal of scandal;
I'll burn what only brings regret . . .
  Kitty, go, fetch a Lighted Candle.
  1856.

INCHBAE.

Anon he shuts the solemn book
--To heed the falling of the brook,
He cares but little why it flows,
Or whence it comes, or where it goes.

For here, on this delightful bank,
His past—his future are a blank ;
Enough for him the bloom, the cheer,
They all are his to-day, and here.

But hark ! a voice that carols free,
And fills the air with melody !
She comes ! a Creature clad in grace,
And joyful promise in her face.

So let her fearlessly intrude
On this his much-loved solitude ;
Is she a lovely phantom, or
That Love he long has waited for ?

O welcome as the morning dew ;
Long, long have I expected you ;
Come, share my seat, and, late or soon,
All else that's mine beneath the moon.

And sing your happy roundelay
While Nature listens.   Till to-day
This mirthful stream has never known
A cadence gladder than its own :

Forgive if I too fondly gaze,
Or praise the eyes that others praise :
I watch'd my Star, I've wander'd far—
Are you my Joy?   You know you are !

Let others praise, as others prize,
The witching twilight of your eyes—
I cannot praise where I adore,
And that is praise—and something more.

THE JESTER'S PLEA.

These verses were published in 1862, in a volume of Poems (by several hands), entitled "An Offering to Lancashire."

The world's a sorry wench, akin
    To all that's frail and frightful :
The world's as ugly, ay, as sin,—
    And almost as delightful !
The world's a merry world (*pro tem.*),
    And some are gay, and therefore
It pleases them, but some condemn
    The world they do not care for.

The world's an ugly world.   Offend
    Good people, how they wrangle !
Their manners that they never mend,—
    The characters they mangle !
They eat, and drink, and scheme, and plod,—
    They go to church on Sunday ;
And many are afraid of God—
    And more of *Mrs. Grundy.*

    *   *   *

The time for pen and sword was when
    " My ladye fayre" for pity
Could tend her wounded knight, and ther
    Be tender to his ditty.
Some ladies now make pretty songs,
    And some make pretty nurses :
Some men are great at righting wrongs,
    And some at writing verses.

I wish we better understood
    The tax our poets levy ;
I know the Muse is *goody-good*,
    I think she's rather heavy :
She now compounds for winning ways
    By morals of the sternest ;
Methinks the lays of nowadays
    Are painfully in earnest.

When wisdom halts, I humb'y try
    To make the most of folly :
If Pallas be unwilling, I
    Prefer to flirt with Polly ;

To quit the goddess for the maid
  Seems low in lofty musers ;
But Pallas is a lofty jade—
  And beggars can't be choosers

    •   •   •   •

I do not wish to see the slaves
  Of party stirring passion,
Or psalms quite superseding staves,
  Or piety " the fashion."
I bless the Hearts where pity glows,
  Who, here together banded,
Are holding out a hand to those
  That wait so empty-handed !

Masters, may one in motley clad,
  A Jester by confession,
Scarce noticed join, half gay, half sad,
  The close of your procession ?
This garment here seems out of place
  With graver robes to mingle,
But if one tear bedews his face,
  Forgive the bells their jingle.

F.

THE ROSE AND THE RING.

(Christmas, 1854, and Christmas, 1863.)

She smiles, but her heart is in sable,
　Ay, sad as her Christmas is chill;
She reads, and her book is the Fable
　He penn'd for her while she was ill.
It is nine years ago since he wrought it,
　Where reedy old Tiber is king;
And chapter by chapter he brought it,
　And read her *The Rose and the Ring.*

And when it was printed, and gaining
　Renown with all lovers of glee,
He sent her this copy containing
　His comical little *croquis;*
A sketch of a rather droll couple,
　She's pretty, he's quite t'other thing!
He begs (with a spine vastly supple)
　She will study *The Rose and the Ring.*

It pleased the kind Wizard to send her
   The last and the best of his Toys;
He aye had a sentiment tender
   For innocent maidens and boys :
And though he was great as a scorner,
   The guileless were safe from his sting :
How sad is past mirth to the mourner—
   A tear on *The Rose and the King!*

She reads; I may vainly endeavour
   Her mirth-chequer'd grief to pursue,
For she knows she has lost, and for ever,
   The heart that was bared to so few ;
But here, on the shrine of his glory,
   One poor little blossom I fling ;
And you see there's a nice little story
   Attach'd to *The Rose and the King.*

1864.

NUPTIAL VERSES.

" Romance can roam not far from home ;
Knock gently, she must answer soon ;
I'm sixty-five, and yet I strive
To hang my garland on the moon."

The town despises modern lays :
   The foolish town is frantic
For story-books that tell of days
   Which time has made romantic ;
Of days, whose chiefest glories fill
   The gloom of crypt and barrow ;
When soldiers were, as Love is still,
   Content with bow and arrow.

But why should we the fancy chide ?
   The world will always hunger
To know how people lived and died
   When all the world was younger.
We like to read of knightly parts
   In maidenhood's distresses,

Of tryst, with sunshine in light hearts ;
  And moonbeam on dark tresses ;

And how, when *errante-knyghte* or *erl*
  Proved well the love he gave her,
·She'd send him scarf or silken curl,
  As earnest of her favour ;
And how (the Fair at times were rude !)
  Her knight, ere homeward riding,
Would take, and, ay with gratitude,
  His lady's silver chiding.

We love the rare old days and rich
  That poetry has painted ;
We mourn those pleasant days with which
  We never were acquainted.
Absurd ! our modern world's divine,
  A world to dare and do in,
A more romantic world.   In fine
  A better world to woo in !

The flow of life is yet a rill
  That laughs, and leaps, and glistens ;
And still the woodland rings, and still
  The old Damœtas listens.

Romance, as tender as she's true,
   Our Isle has never quitted :
So, LAD and LASSIE, when you woo,
   You hardly need be pitied.

Our lot is cast on pleasant days,
   In not unpleasant places ;
Young ladies now have pretty ways,
   As well as pretty faces ;
So never sigh for what has been,
   And let us cease complaining
That we have loved when our dear Queen
   VICTORIA was reigning.

Oh yes, young love is lovely yet,
   With faith and honour plighted :
I love to see a pair so met,
   Youth—Beauty—all united.
Such Dear Ones may they ever wear
   The roses fortune gave them :
Ah, know we such a BLESSED PAIR ?
   I think we do ! GOD SAVE THEM !

AN OLD BUFFER.

BUFFER.—A cushion or apparatus, with strong springs, to deaden the buff or concussion between a moving body and one on which it strikes.—*Webster's English Dictionary.*

> "*If Blossom's a sceptic, or saucy, I'll search,*
> *And I'll find her a wholesome corrective—in Church!*"
>   MAMMA *loquitur.*

"A knock-me-down sermon, and worthy of
        Birch,"
Says I to my Wife, as we toddle from church;
"Convincing indeed!" is the lady's remark;
"How logical, too, on the size of the Ark!"
Then Blossom cut in, without begging our
        pardons,
"Pa, was it as big as the 'Logical Gardens?"

"Miss Blossom," says I to my dearest of Dearies,
"Papa disapproves of nonsensical queries;
The Ark was an Ark, and had people to build it,
Enough that we're told Noah built it and fill'd it:

Mamma doesn't ask how he caught his opossums.'
—Said she, "That remark is as foolish as
   Blossom's ! "

Thus talking and walking, the time is beguiled
By my orthodox Wife and my sceptical Child ;
I act as their *buffer*, whenever I can,
And you see I'm of use as a family man.
I parry their blows, and I've plenty to do—
I think that the Child's are the worst of the two !

My Wife has a healthy aversion for sceptics,
She vows they are bad—why, they're only dys-
   peptics !
May Blossom prove neither the one nor the other,
But do as she's bid by her excellent mother.
She thinks I'm a Solon ; perhaps, if I huff her,
She'll think I'm a. . . Something that's denser and
   tougher.

MANY YEARS AFTER.

ANOTHER POET SPEAKS.

(See Note.)

I saw some books exposed for sale—
Some dear, and some—stage-play and tale—
  As dear as any :
A few, perhaps more orthodox
Or torn, were tumbled in a box—
  'All these a penny.'

I open'd one at hazard, but
Its leaves, though soil'd, were still uncut ;
  And yet before
I'd read a page, I felt indeed
A wish to cut that leaf, and read
  Some pages more.

A Poet sang of what befel
When, years gone by, he'd paced Pall Mall :
  While walking thus—

A Boy—he'd met a Maiden.   Then
Fair women all were brave, and men
       Were virtuous !

They oft had met, he wonder'd why ;
He praised her sprightly air, and I
       Believe he meant it :
They never spoke, but if he smiled
Her eyes had seem'd to say (poor Child !)
       ' I don't resent it.'

And then this Poet mused and grieved,
In kindly strain, his Verse relieved
       By kindlier jest :
Then he, with sad, prophetic glance,
Bethought him she, ere then, perchance
       Had found her rest.

Then I was minded how my Joy
Sometimes had told me of a Boy
       With curly head—
' You know,' she'd laugh—(she then was well !)
' I used to meet him in Pall Mall,
       Ere you me wed.'

And then, for fun, she'd vow, ' Good lack,
I'll go there now and fetch thee back
> At least a curl ! '
She once was here, now she is gone !
And so, you see, *my* Wife was yon
> Bright little Girl !

I am not one for shedding tears ;
That Boy's now dead, or bow'd with years ;
> But see—*sometimes*
He'd thought of Her !—that made me weep ;
That's why I bought—and why I keep
> His Book of Rhymes.

1872

GERALDINE GREEN.

I.

THE SERENADE.

If pathos should thy bosom stir
To tears more sweet than laughter,
Then bless its kind interpreter,
And love him ever after !

Light slumber is quitting
　　The eyelids it prest ;
The fairies are flitting,
　　Who lull'd thee to rest.
Where night dews were falling,
　　Now feeds the wild bee ;
The starling is calling,
　　My Darling, for thee.

The wavelets are crisper
　　That thrill the shy fern ;
The leaves fondly whisper,
　　" We wait thy return."

Arise then, and hazy
   Regrets from thee fling,
For sorrows that crazy
   To-morrows may bring:

A vague yearning smote us,
   But wake not to weep ;
My bark, Love, shall float us
   Across the still deep,
To isles where the lotus
   Erst lull'd thee to sleep.

1861.

II.

MY LIFE IS A ——,

At Worthing, an exile from Geraldine G——,
How aimless, how wretched an Exile is he !
Promenades are not even prunella and leather
To lovers, if lovers can't foot them together.

He flies the parade, by the ocean he stands ;
He traces a " Geraldine G." on the sands ;

Only "G.!" though her loved patronymic is
    "Green,"—
"I will not betray thee, my own Geraldine."

— The fortunes of men have a time and a tide,
And Fate, the old Fury, will not be denied;
That name was, of course, soon wiped out by the
    sea,—
She jilted the Exile, did Geraldine G.

They meet, but they never have spoken since that;
He hopes she is happy,—he knows she is fat;
She, woo'd on the shore, now is wed in the Strand;
And *I*—it was I wrote her name on the sand.
    1854.

FROM THE CRADLE.

They tell me I was born a long
 Three months ago,
But whether they be right or wrong
 I hardly know.
I sleep, I smile, I cannot crawl,
 But I can cry:
At present I am rather small—
 A Babe am I.

The changing lights of sun and shade
 Are baby toys;
The flowers and birds are not afraid
 Of baby-boys.
Some day I'll wish that I could be
 A bird and fly;
At present I can't wish—you see
 A Babe am I.

THE TWINS.

Yes, there they lie, so small, so quaint,
　　Two mouths, two noses, and two chins;
What Painter shall we get to paint
　　And glorify the Twins?
To give us all the charm that dwells
In tiny cloaks and coral-bells,
And all those other pleasant spells
Of Babyhood, and not forget
The silver mug for either Pet—
　　No babe should be without it?
Come, Fairy Limner! you can thrill
Our hearts with pink and daffodil,
And white rosette, and dimpled frill;
Come, paint our little Jack and Jill,
　　And don't be long about it!

THE OLD CRADLE.

And this was your Cradle? Why, surely, my
    Jenny,
  Such cosy dimensions go clearly to show
You were an exceedingly small Picaninny
  Some nineteen or twenty short summers ago.

Your baby-days flow'd in a much-troubled
    channel;
  I see you, as then, in your impotent strife,
A tight little bundle of wailing and flannel,
  Perplex'd with the newly-found fardel of Life.

To hint at an infantile frailty's a scandal;
  Let bygones be bygones, for somebody knows
It was bliss such a Baby to dance and to
    dandle,—
  Your cheeks were so dimpled, so rosy your
    toes!

F

Ay, here is your Cradle; and Hope, a bright
        spirit,
    With Love now is watching beside it, I know.
They guard the wee Nest It was yours to inherit
    Some nineteen or twenty short summers ago.

It is Hope gilds the future, Love welcomes it
        smiling;
    Thus wags this old World, therefore stay not
        to ask,
"My future bids fair, is my future beguiling?"
    If mask'd, still it pleases—then raise not its
        mask.

Is Life a poor coil some would gladly be doffing?
    He is riding post-haste who their wrongs will
        adjust;
For at most 'tis a footstep from cradle to coffin—
    From a spoonful of pap to a mouthful of dust.

Then smile as your future is smiling, my Jenny;
    I see you, except for those infantine woes,

Little changed since you were but a small Pica-
    ninny—
Your cheeks were so dimpled, so rosy your toes!

Ay, here is your Cradle, much, much to my liking,
    Though nineteen or twenty long winters have
    sped.
Hark ! As I'm talking there's six o'clock striking, —
    It is time JENNY'S BABY should be in its bed.

    1885

LOVE, TIME, AND DEATH.

Ah me, dread friends of mine—Love, Time, and
    Death !
  Sweet Love, who came to me on sheeny wing,
And gave her to my arms—her lips, her breath,
  And all her golden ringlets clustering :
And Time who gathers in the flying years,
  He gave me all, but where is all he gave ?
He took my Love and left me barren tears,
  Weary and lone I follow to the grave.
There Death will end this vision half divine,—
  Wan Death, who waits in shadow evermore,
And silent, ere he give the sudden sign.
  O, gently lead me thro' thy narrow door,
Thou gentle Death, thou trustiest friend of mine--
  Ah me, for Love . . . *will* Death my love
    restore ?

AN EPITAPH.

Her worth, her wit, her loving smile
  Were with me but a little while;
She came, she went; yet though that Voice
Is hush'd that made the heart rejoice,
And though the grave is dark and chill,
Her memory is fragrant still,—
She stands on the eternal hill.

Here pause, kind soul, whoe'er you be,
And weep for her, and pray for me.

BABY MINE.

Baby mine, with the grave, grave face,
 Where did you get that royal calm,
Too staid for joy, too still for grace?
 I bend as I kiss your pink, soft palm;
Are you the first of a nobler race,
     Baby mine?

You come from the region of *long ago*,
 And gazing awhile where the seraphs dwell
Has given your face a glory and glow—
 Of that brighter land have you aught to tell
I seem to have known it—I more would know,
     Baby mine.

Your calm, blue eyes have a far-off reach,
 Look at me now with those wondrous eyes,
Why are we doom'd to the gift of speech
 While you are silent, and sweet, and wise?
You have much to learn—you have more to teach,
     Baby mine.

DU RYS DE MADAME D'ALLEBRET.

How fair those locks which now the light-wind stirs!
　　What eyes she has, and what a perfect arm !
And yet methinks that little Laugh of hers—
　　That little Laugh is still her crowning charm.
Where'er she passes, countryside or town,
　　The streets make festa, and the fields rejoice.
Should sorrow come, as 't will, to cast me down,
　　Or Death, as come he must, to hush my voice,
Her Laugh would wake me, just as now it thrills
　　　　me—
That little giddy Laugh wherewith she kills me.

THE LADY I LOVE.

The Lady I sing is as charming as Spring,
I own that I love the dear Lady I sing :
She is gay, she is sad, she is good, she is fair,
She lives at a Number in — — — Square.

It is not 21, it is not 23—
You never shall get at her Number from me ;
If you did, very soon you'd be mounting the stair
Of Number (no matter what !) — — — Square.

They say she is clever.   Indeed it is said
She is making a Novel right out of her Head !
That poor little Head ! If her Heart were to spare
I'd break, and I'd mend it in — — — Square.

I've a heart of my own, and, in prose as in rhymes,
This heart has been fractured a good many times ;
An excellent heart, tho' in sorry repair—
Little Friend, may I mend it in — — — *Square !*

" *What nonsense you talk.*" Yes, but still I am one
Who feels pretty grave when he seems full of fun ;
Some people are pretty, and yet full of care—
And Some One is pretty in — — — Square.

I know I am singing in old-fashion'd phrase
The music that pleased in the old-fashion'd days ;
Alas, I know, too, I've an old-fashion'd air—
Oh, why did I ever see — — — Square !

POSTSCRIPT.

The writer of prose, by intelligence taught,
Says the thing that will please, in the way that he ought
But your poor despised Bard, who by Nature is blest,
(In the scope of a couplet, or guise of a jest,)
Says the thing that he pleases as pleases him best.

OUR PHOTOGRAPHS.

She play'd me false, but that's not why
I haven't quite forgiven Di,
    Although I've tried :
This curl was hers, so brown, so bright,
She gave it me one blissful night,
    And—more beside !

Our photographs were group'd together ;
She wore the darling hat and feather
    That I adore ;
In profile by her side I sat
Reading my poetry—but that
    She'd heard before.

Why, after all, Di threw me over
I never knew, I can't discover,
    And hardly guess ;
May be Smith's lyrics she decided
Were sweeter than the sweetest I did—
    I acquiesce.

A week before their wedding day,
That Beast was call'd in haste away
     To join the Staff.
Di gave him then, with tearful mien,
Her only photograph. I've seen
     That photograph,

I've seen it in Smith's pocket-book !
Just think ! her hat, her tender look,
     Are now that Brute's !
Before she gave it, off she cut
My body, head, and lyrics, but
She was obliged, the little Slut,
     To leave my Boots.

MY FIRST-BORN.

" He shan't be their namesake, the rather
    That both are such opulent men :
His name shall be that of his father,
    My Benjamin, shorten'd to *Ben.*

" Yes, *Ben,* though it cost him a portion
    In each of my relatives' wills :
I scorn such baptismal extortion—
    (That creaking of boots must be Squills.)

" It is clear, though his means may be narrow,
    This infant his Age will adorn ;
I shall send him to Oxford from Harrow,—
    I wonder how soon he'll be born ! "

A spouse thus was airing his fancies
    Below, 'twas a labour of love,
And was calmly reflecting on Nancy's
    More practical labour above ;

Yet while it so pleased him to ponder,
　Elated, at ease, and alone ;
That pale, patient victim up yonder
　Had budding delights of her own :

.Sweet thoughts, in their essence diviner
　Than paltry ambition and pelf ;
A cherub, no babe will be finer !
　Invented and nursed by herself ;

At breakfast, and dining, and teaing,
　An appetite nought can appease,
And quite a Young-Reasoning-Being
　When call'd on to yawn and to sneeze.

What cares that heart, trusting and tender,
　For fame or avuncular wills ?
Except for the name and the gender,
　She's almost as tranquil as Squills.

That father, in reverie centred,
　Dumbfounder'd, his thoughts in a whirl,
Heard Squills, as the creaking boots enter'd,
　Announce that his Boy was—a Girl.

MR. PLACID'S FLIRTATION.

Jemima was cross, and I lost my umbrella
That day at the tomb of Cecilia Metella.
LETTERS FROM ROME.

Miss Tristram's *poulet* ended thus: " Nota bene,
We meet for croquet in the Aldobrandini."
Says my wife, " Then I'll drive, and you'll ride
    with Selina "
(Jones's fair spouse, of the Via Sistina).

We started : I'll own that my family deem
I'm an ass, but I'm not quite the ass that I seem ;
As we cross'd the stones gently a nursemaid said
    " La—
There goes Mrs. Jones with Miss Placid's papa ! "

Our friends, one or two may be mention'd anon,
Had arranged *rendezvous* at the Gate of St. John :

That pass'd, off we spun over turf that's not green
    there,
And soon were all met at the villa. You've been
    there ?

I'll try and describe, or I won't, if you please,
The cheer that was set for us under the trees :
You have read the *menu*, may you read it again ;
Champagne, perigord, galantine, and—champagne.

Suffice it to say, I got seated between
Mrs. Jones and old Brown—to the latter's chagrin.
Poor Brown, who believes in himself, and—another
    thing,
Whose talk is so bald, but whose cheeks are so—
    t'other thing.

She sang, her sweet voice fill'd the gay garden
    alleys ;
I jested, but Brown would not smile at my sallies ;—
(Selina remark'd that a swell met at Rome
Is not always a swell when you meet him at home.)

The luncheon despatch'd, we adjourn'd to croquet,
A dainty, but difficult sport in its way.
Thus I counsel the sage, who to play at it stoops,
Belabour thy neighbour, and spoon through thy
   hoops.

Then we stroll'd, and discourse found its kindest
   of tones :
"How charming were solitude and—Mrs. Jones ! '
" Indeed, Mr. Placid, I dote on the sheeny
And shadowy paths of the Aldobrandini !"

A girl came with violet posies, and two
Soft eyes, like her violets, freshen'd with dew,
And a kind of an indolent, fine-lady air,—
As if she by accident found herself there.

I bought one.   Selina was pleased to accept it ;
She gave me a rosebud to keep—and I've kept it.
Then twilight was near, and I think, in my heart,
When she vow'd she must go, she was loth to
   depart.

Cattivo momento! we dare not delay :
The steeds are remounted, and wheels roll away :
The ladies *condemn* Mrs. Jones, as the phrase is,
But vie with each other in chanting my praises.

"He has so much to say!" cries the fair Mrs.
     Legge ;
" How amusing he was about missing the peg ! "
" What a beautiful smile ! " says the plainest Miss
     Gunn.
All echo, " He's charming ! delightful !—What
     fun ! "

This sounds rather *nice,* and it's perfectly clear it
Had sounded more *nice* had I happen'd to hear it ;
The men were less civil, and gave me a rub,
So I happen'd to hear when I went to the Club.

Says Brown, " I shall drop Mr. Placid's society ;
(Brown is a prig of improper propriety ;)
" Hang him," said Smith (who from cant's not
     exempt)
" Why he'll bring immorality into contempt."

G

Says I (to myself) when I found me alone,
" My wife has my heart, is it always her own ?"
And further, says I (to myself) " I'll be shot
If I know if Selina adores me or not."

Says Jones, " I've just come from the *scavi*, at Veii,
And I've bought some remarkably fine scarabæi ! "

ST. GEORGE'S, HANOVER SQUARE.

She pass'd up the aisle on the arm of her sire,
A delicate lady in bridal attire,
　　Fair emblem of virgin simplicity;
Half London was there, and, my word, there were
　　　few
That stood by the altar, or hid in a pew,
　　But envied Lord Nigel's felicity.

Beautiful Bride! So meek in thy splendour,
So frank in thy love, and its trusting surrender,
　　Departing you leave us the town dim!
May happiness wing to thy bower, unsought,
And may Nigel, esteeming his bliss as he ought,
　　Prove worthy thy worship,—confound him!

MA FUTURE.

We parted, but again I stopt
    To greet her at the door,
Her thimble, mine the gift, had dropt
    Unheeded to the floor.

Her eyes met mine, her eyelids fell
    To veil their sweet content ;
Her happy blush and kind *farewell*
    Were with me as I went.

And when I join'd the human tide
    And turmoil of the street,
A Spirit-form was at my side,
    And gladness wing'd my feet.

Exultingly the world went by,
    The town and I were gay !
And one far stretch of soft blue sky
    Seem'd leading me away.

I left her happy, and I know
   That we shall meet anon ;
I left my Love an hour ago,
   And yet she is not gone.

VANITY FAIR.

"Vanitas vanitatum" has rung in the ears
Of gentle and simple for thousands of years;
The wail still is heard, yet its notes never scare
Either simple or gentle from Vanity Fair.

I often hear people abusing it, yet
There the young go to learn and the old to forget;
The mirth may be feigning, the sheen may be glare,
But the gingerbread's gilded in Vanity Fair.

Old Dives there rolls in his chariot, but mind
Black Care has crept up with the lacqueys behind;
Joan trudges with Jack,—are the Sweethearts aware
Of the trouble that waits them in Vanity Fair?

We saw them all go, and we something may learn
Of the harvest they reap when we see them return;
The tree was enticing, its branches are bare,—
Heigho for the promise of Vanity Fair.

That stupid old Dives, once honest enough,
His honesty sold for star, ribbon, and stuff;
And Joan's pretty face has been clouded with care
Since Jack bought her ribbons at Vanity Fair.

Contemptible Dives! too credulous Joan!
Yet we all have a Vanity Fair of our own;
My son, you have yours, but you need not despair—
I own I've a weakness for Vanity Fair.

Philosophy halts—wise counsels are vain,
We go, we repent, we return there again;
To-night you will certainly meet with us there—
So come and be merry in Vanity Fair.

1850.

MY NEIGHBOUR'S WIFE!

Hark !   Hark to my neighbour's flute !
Yon powder'd slave, that ox, that ass are his:
Hark to his wheezy pipe ; my neighbour is
    A worthy sort of brute.

    My tuneful neighbour's rich—has houses, lands,
A wife (confound his flute)—a handsome wife !
Her love must give a gusto to his life.
      See yonder—there she stands.

    She turns, she gazes, she has lustrous eyes,
A throat like Juno, and Aurora's arms—
Per Bacco, what a paragon of charms !
      My neighbour's drawn a prize.

    Yet, somehow, life's a nuisance with its woes,
Disease and doubt—and that eternal preaching :
We've suffer'd from our early pious teaching—
      We suffer   goodness knows.

How vain the wealth that breeds its own
    vexation !
Yet few of us would care to quite forego it :
Then weariness of life—and many know it—
    Is not a glad sensation :

And, therefore, neighbour mine, without a
    sting
I contemplate thy fields, thy house, thy flocks,
I covet not thy man, thine ass, thine ox,
    Thy flute, thy—anything.

ARCADY.

LIVELY SHEPHERDESS.

Now mind,
He'll call on you to-morrow at eleven,
And beg that you will dine with us at seven;
If, when He calls, you see that He has got
His green umbrella, then you'll know He'll not
Be going to the House, and you'll decline,
But if He hasn't it, you'll come and dine.

HAPPY SHEPHERD.

But if it rains : then how? and where? and when?
And how about the green umbrella then?

LIVELY SHEPHERDESS.

Then He'll be Wet, that's all, for if I don't
Choose He should take it, why, of course! you
goose! he won't.

MABEL'S MUFF.

She's jealous !   Does it grieve me ?   No !
I'm glad to see my Mabel so,
  Carina mia !
Poor Puss !   That now and then she draws
Conclusions, not without a cause,
  Is my idea.

She loves ; and I'm prepared to prove
That jealousy is kin to love
  In constant women.
My jealous Pussy cut up rough
The day before I bought her muff
  With sable trimming.

These tearful darlings think to quell us
By being so divinely jealous ;
  But I know better.
Hillo !   Who's that !   A damsel !   Come,
I'll follow :—no, I can't, for some
  One else has met her.

What fun !   He looks "a lad of grace."
She holds her muff to hide her face ;
    They kiss,—The Sly Puss !
Hillo ! Her muff,—it's trimm'd with sable ! .
It's like the muff I gave to Mabel ! . . .
    Goodl-o-r-d, SHE'S *MY* PUSS !

A KIND PROVIDENCE.

He dropt a tear on Susan's bier,
 He seem'd a most despairing Swain;
But bluer sky brought newer tie,
 And—would he wish her back again?
The moments fly, and when we die,
 Will Philly Thistletop complain?
She'll cry and sigh, and—dry her eye,
 And let herself be woo'd again.

NOTES.

NOTES

"A Winter Fantasy."

The two first stanzas are imitated from Théophile Gautier.

"To My Old Friend Postumus."

The Well-beloved !—B. L. died 26th July, 1853.

"The Rose and the Ring."

Mr. Thackeray spent a portion of the winter of 1854 in Rome, and while there he wrote his little Christmas story called "The Rose and the Ring." He was a great friend of the distinguished American sculptor, Mr. Story, and was a frequent visitor at his house. I have heard Mr. Story speak with emotion of the kindness of Mr. Thackeray to his little daughter, then recovering from a severe illness, and he told me that Mr. Thackeray used to come nearly every day to read to Miss Story, often bringing portions of his manuscript with him.

Five or six years afterwards Miss Story showed me a very pretty copy of "The Rose and the King," which Mr. Thackeray had sent her, with a facetious sketch of himself in the act of presenting her with the work.

"NUPTIAL VERSES."

These lines were published in 1863 in "A Welcome," dedicated to the Princess of Wales.

"MANY YEARS AFTER."

These lines are intended as a sequel to my verses in "London Lyrics," entitled "The Pilgrims of Pall Mall."

"DU RYS DE MADAME D'ALLEBRET."

After Clément Marot.

"ST. GEORGE'S, HANOVER SQUARE."

"Dans le bonheur de nos meilleurs amis nous trouvons souvent quelque chose qui ne nous plaît pas entièrement."